On the Menu

Written by Jill Eggleton
Illustrated by Brent Chambers

Felix Brown collects menus. They are not just ordinary menus. They are interesting ones. He goes all over the world looking for menus. He likes to find out what can be eaten.

The Desert Cafe

MENU

Starters
A Bowl of Nuts from the Mungo Tree
Ostrich Soup
Grilled Porcupine Spikes

•

Mains
Roasted Lizard with Dried Seeds
Barbecued Bugs

•

Dessert
Honey Pot Ants

•

Drinks
Camel Milk
Cold Tea

You will love the Desert Cafe. It has real rock tables and chairs, and all the food is served on cactus plates.

THE IGLOO EATING HOUSE

Winter Menu

Fresh Seal Meat
Dried Walrus
Smoked Fish
Fox Stew

Summer Menu

Fresh Fish
Goose Stew
Bird Eggs Served Raw
Berries

The Igloo Eating House is open all year, unless closed by snowstorms. Food is served in bowls made from ice. You need to wear gloves to eat your food!

The Alley Cat Corner Cafe

Breakfast
Sausage Skins

Lunch
Drips of Milkshake
Old Egg Sandwich

Dinner
Crust of Dry Bread
Lick of Tuna Tin

Drinks
Puddle Water
(available if raining)

The Alley Cat Corner Cafe is open every day. All meals are served on the sidewalk outside the cafe or under the cafe steps. No reservations are taken because the food disappears quickly.

Poodle Paradise Diner

Breakfast

Bacon, eggs, and hot potato cake
with tomato sauce
Pancakes with chocolate
and cream
Coconut milk or hot chocolate

Lunch

Tuna fish sandwiches served with bacon bits

Dinner

Starter
Sausage soup with bone chips

Main
Meat with mashed potatoes
and mushroom gravy

Dessert
Raspberry ice cream and blueberry jelly

The Poodle Paradise Diner opens daily at 6pm. All meals are served on silver plates. Reservations are required.

Crazy Cafe

Dinner

Starters
Snail soup served in a sieve

Mains
Raspberry fritters and chicken legs
in ice-cream gravy
(served hot on a paper plate)

Dessert
Potato chip pudding served upside down
with tomato cream

B.Y.O.C.

The Crazy Cafe opens at 5 o'clock in the morning. Round, oblong, or triangle tables are available. It is a B.Y.O.C. restaurant (that means you bring your own chair).

Terry's Take-outs

Bird Bar

Toasted seeds wrapped in spider webs

Grass salad with ant dressing

Lizard shakes

Mouse Meals

Cheese chips

Mouse burgers

Cake-crumb pudding and mouse cream

Dog Dinners

Meat pie

Bone burgers

Terry's Take-outs has food for everyone. They are open all hours.

16

I stick the menus that I collect all over the walls of my house. My menus are more interesting than wallpaper. When I get hungry, I read the walls. After I have read the walls, I'm not hungry anymore. It is amazing what can be eaten. No wonder some stomachs moan and groan!

Food Menus

Purpose: to list and describe food dishes

How to Write a Food Menu:

Step One
Think about the foods you want on your menu. Make a list of the foods.

Pizza
Fruit salad
Roast chicken
Pancakes
Fish and fries
Spaghetti
Apple pie

Step Two
Decide what headings your menu will have. You could start with:
Breakfast
Lunch
Dinner

Or you could choose headings such as:
Starters
Mains
Desserts
Drinks

Step Three
**Look at your
list of foods.
Put the dishes
under the right
heading.**

MENU
Breakfast
Pancakes
Lunch
Pizza
Fruit salad
Dinner
Roast chicken
Fish and fries
Spaghetti
Apple pie

**(You could also write how much each dish
will cost.)**

Step Four
**Now you could write a short description for
each dish. You could say what is in the dish
and how it tastes.**

MENU
Breakfast
Pancakes filled with berries-very sweet
Lunch
Pizza with tomato and mushroom –
delicious

*Remember: You can
use interesting letters
and designs to make
your menu look great!*

19

▬▬▬ Guide Notes

Title: On the Menu
Stage: Fluency (2)

Text Form: Menus
Approach: Guided Reading
Processes: Thinking Critically, Exploring Language, Processing Information
Written and Visual Focus: Menus, Speech Bubbles

THINKING CRITICALLY
(sample questions)
- Why do you think there is camel milk on the Desert Cafe menu and not cow's milk?
- Why do you think there are old egg sandwiches at the Alley Cat Corner Cafe?
- What is the difference between the menus at the Poodle Paradise Diner and the Alley Cat Corner Cafe?
- How do you think the Crazy Cafe got its name?

EXPLORING LANGUAGE

Terminology
Spread, author and illustrator credits, ISBN number

Vocabulary
Clarify: available, menu, paradise, stale, sieve
Nouns: cafe, diner, menu, lunch
Verbs: serve, wear, bring, lick, wrap
Singular/plural: lunch/lunches, potato/potatoes
Abbreviations: B.Y.O.C. (Bring your own chair), pm (*post meridiem* – past morning)

Print Conventions
Dash, apostrophe – possessive (Terry's Take-outs)
Parenthesis: (served hot on a paper plate), (available if raining)